Scholastic Press
345 Pacific Highway Lindfield NSW 2070
An imprint of Scholastic Australia Pty Limited (ABN 11 000 614 577)
PO Box 579 Gosford NSW 2250
www.scholastic.com.au

Part of the Scholastic Group
Sydney • Auckland • New York • Toronto • London • Mexico City
• New Delhi • Hong Kong • Buenos Aires • Puerto Rico

First published by Scholastic Australia in 2013.
Text copyright © Anh Do, 2013.
Illustrations copyright © Jules Faber, 2013.

National Library of Australia Cataloguing-in-Publication entry
Author: Do, Anh, author.
Title: WeirDo / written by Anh Do ; illustrated by Jules Faber.
ISBN: 9781742837581 (paperback)
Target Audience: For primary school age.
Other Authors/Contributors: Faber, Jules, 1971-, illustrator.
Dewey Number: A823.4

Typeset in Grenadine MVB, Push Ups and Lunch Box.

Printed by RR Donnelley.
Scholastic Australia's policy, in association with RR
Donnelley, is to use papers that are renewable and
made efficiently from wood grown in sustainable forests,
so as to minimise its environmental footprint.

BLAH,
BLAH,
BLAH

10 9

17 / 1

ANH DO

Illustrated by JULES FABER

WEiRDO

A SCHOLASTIC PRESS BOOK
FROM SCHOLASTIC AUSTRALIA

CHAPTER 1

Here we go again. Even in a **new school**, in a **new town**, my year is about to start the **exact** same way it always does ...

WHAT'S YOUR NAME?

WEIR.

'That's an interesting name. What's your surname?' says Miss Franklin.

That's the bit I **really** hate. Why does **everyone** have to ask for your **surname**?

'Weir, what's your surname?' she asks again.

DO.

DO?
RHYMES WITH
'GO'?

UH-HUH . . .

'Your name's . . . Weir *Do*? It's not really, is it?'

'Yes, actually, it is,' I reply.

WEIRDO?

Get ready for it. In exactly **three** seconds, all the kids will start laughing . . .

That's the story of my life!

SO WHAT'S YOUR SISTER'S
NAME? PLAY?

→ PLAY DO!

HA HA HA

WHAT'S YOUR FATHER'S
NAME? TAE KWON?

↝ TAEKWONDO!

HA HA HA

What I would give for a surname like **Smith** or **Jones** or **Chapman** or **Fletcher**. Anything! Even **GoopGoop** goes better with Weir than Do.

What's your name?

Weir GOOPGOOP!

YAY!

I guess when they gave out surnames,

I lost ... big time.

Here we go,
Weir...

Let's see
what your
surname
will be...

Thing is, my dad was born in Vietnam. His last name is **Do**. (Yep, rhymes with go.)

My mum's last name before she married my dad was **Weir**. She really loved that name, so I got lumped with Weir Do! **WEIRDO!**

Lucky Me!

My parents could have given me any first name at all, like **John, Kevin, Shmevin,**

ANYTHING!

What about Rusty? **Rusty Do** sounds like a movie star.

I'd like to thank my parents for my cool name!

Or maybe a famous country music singer.

I'm glad I'm not a Weirdooooooooooo

Instead I'm stuck with the **worst** name since **Mrs Face** called her son **Bum**.

Now that was a **funny** roll call:

☑ **Kevin Clark**
☑ **Mary Connors**
☐ **Bum Face**

HAHA HA HA

Anyway, back to class ...

'Children, it's **rude** to laugh at someone's name,' says the teacher. 'I'm sorry, Weir ... *Do*. Please sit down, Weir ... DO.'

And then it started.

I could tell the teacher was trying **really hard** not to laugh. It's a sign when people's cheeks puff up like they're about to **explode**.

I'm actually an expert on the subject.
I've seen it **a lot**.

My Kindergarten teacher

My Year One teacher

Finally my new teacher ran out of the classroom...

BWA HA HAHA HAHAHA HA HAHA!

then she returned.

PLEASE TAKE A SEAT, WEIR . . .

I was so busy trying not to look embarrassed,
I forgot I was wearing my sister's old shoes . . .

and

tripped.

That's when a **girl** reached down

to help me up.

As I looked into her face, I thought she was the

 <u>most</u> **beautiful**

girl in the world.

Her pencil case read,

Bella Allen.

CHAPTER 2

I guess I should tell you a bit about my family.

My sister's name is Sally.

Why did *she* get the normal name? Not that I'd like to be called Sally.

Sally Do

Me

Sally is older than me by three years and she is one of those people who always saves up her Easter eggs for months and months. It used to be great finding her **hidden** pile of eggs in **June!**

But last year she'd had enough of me eating her stash, so she invented a way to make sure I **never** touched them **again**.

Sally also likes to bug me with some <u>really</u> annoying habits.

Then Dad gave me some tips on how to get her back.

But then she figured out a way around it.

Sally's also one of those people who

<u>**always**</u> makes her bed ...

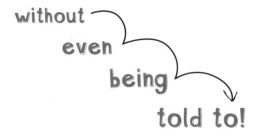

In fact, almost **everything** she does makes me look **bad.**

Sally's wardrobe

My wardrobe

Sally's homework

My homework

My little brother's name is **Roger**.

Another normal name, but read on ⟫⟫

he's **NOT** normal.

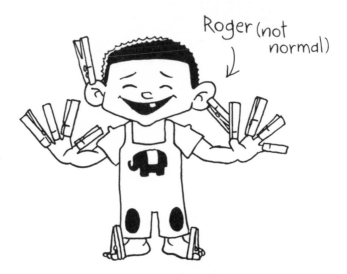

Roger (not normal)

He has just become tall enough to use the toilet instead of his potty. But it's not going so well so far. For the **third time** this week, he's slammed the toilet seat on his **thing** ...

He's also been dipping stuff in his baby food.
Often **stuff that is important.**

PHONE WANT
EAT CUSTARD?

Roger is just starting to talk, and some words come out **funny**. Like when he tries to say **Father**, it sounds more like something else.

SAY 'FATHER'

SAY 'BIG FATHER!'

BIG FARTER!

BIG FARTER! BIG FARTER!

Big Farter is actually a good way to describe Dad.

My dad is one of those dads who tells you not to **pass wind** in public, but then when he feels like it, he just goes ahead and **FARTS**.

RRRRRIIPPP!!!

If Mum's nearby, Dad will try to blame it on something else that **couldn't possibly** have made such a **big** noise.

Like...

But if Mum's not around and it's just us kids,
Dad likes to **boast**.

And here's a tip, if my dad ever asks you to pull his finger ...

DON'T!

Just run the other way!

PULL MY
FINGER . . .

If you're **too slow**, it's time to
get out the **clothes pegs**.

Here's my mum. She's one of those people who **loves** to save money. I don't want to call her **cheap** ... but she is.

She won't even let me change the water after Roger has a bath. And if Roger's been playing in the **dirt** all day, I reckon I come out **dirtier** than when I went in.

But **the worst** thing she does is she **licks** her hand to **fix up my hair.**

WEIR, COME HERE, YOU'VE GOT A HAIR OUT OF PLACE.

SLURP!

Great. Now I look like the **world's biggest nerd** and **smell** like the **tuna sandwich** Mum had at lunch.

Mum's cheap-ness also explains why I was wearing **my sister's shoes** on the first day of school.

They don't really fit yet, but Mum says they will encourage my feet to grow.

As if shoes
speak to feet!

The **craziest** person in our family is **Granddad**.
He is Mum's dad and he is

really, really, really old.

He is so old, sometimes bits of him just fall out.

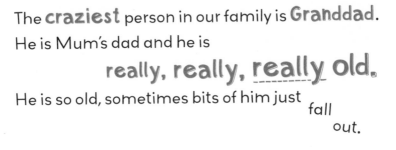

But he always pops
everything back in place.

SQUELCH!

If I got to choose robotic parts, I'd get some **really fast legs**. Cos I'm not a very fast runner. When they handed out **fast running**, I lost out.

I lost out on **tall-ness**, too.

And on **good hair**.

I'm a bit different, I won't lie. WEIRDO's not just my name. It kind of describes the way I am . . .

Like whenever I eat a hamburger, the meat **always** falls out the bottom. I hate that.

And whenever I pull off a bandaid, I always **rip off my scab** too.

I can't eat the **stringy** stuff on the inside of a banana. That stuff tastes **strange**.

But **I LIKE** lots of weird things too, like when it's **hot** at night, and you turn your pillow over, the other side is **nice and COOL!**

Like an **extra** pillow! **I love that!**

I also like it when you have to **PEE REALLY BADLY** and you find a toilet just in time.

AAAAAHH!

Or when there's an ad break on your **favourite** TV show, and you run out to do something really important but then you come back **just in time!**

It's also great when you mix up a packet of **cheesy macaroni**, and half way through eating it, you get that one

bright orange macaroni bit

with

stacks of flavour

stuck on it!

YAY!

But most of all, **I love to draw!**

I like drawing

anything,

anywhere.

I even like drawing on the steamy mirror after a bath.

What I like drawing the most are animals. **Not just any animals,** but

WEIRD animals.

I like to mix them up!

My favourite is a **Duck** crossed with a **Poodle**:

Duck + Poodle
= DOODLE!

Or a **Fish** crossed with a **Cat**:

Fish + Cat
= FAT!

Or a **Frog** crossed with a **Pug**:

Frog + Pug
= FRUG!

At the end of the day, things aren't too bad.
There are some things that I'm **GOOD AT**.

Like **spelling** ...

And **remembering people's names**.

I do this by making a picture in my mind of
something that **rhymes** with a person's name.

Like I remembered the name of a girl from my
old school called **Alana Stead**
by thinking of the words
Banana Head.

Of course **Mrs Face's**
kid is **easy!**

Bum Face

CHAPTER 3

Let's get back to my first day in my new school.

The bell rang for little lunch and I followed everyone out into the playground.

I could see it was a normal playground with all the normal silliness.

HOW TO:
Smell the cheese

BOOYAH!

I can't believe some kids still fall for that!

HOW TO: Arm Burn

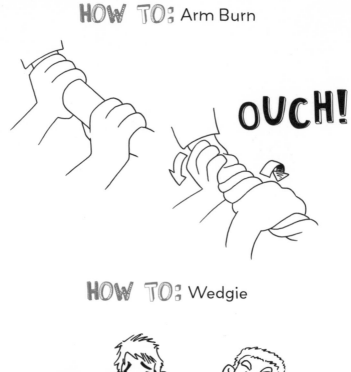

OUCH!

HOW TO: Wedgie

EEK!

HOW TO: shoe lacing.

WHOA!

I looked over to the corner and saw *Bella Allen* sitting with another girl from our class. It looked like she was about to get a

Wet Willy in her ear!

I rushed over to save her but **tripped** and **fell** again!

Stupid shoes!

So I called out from the ground...

BELLA! WATCH OUT!

She turned and—

WET
WILLY!

Oh, **NO!** I just caused Bella to get a
poke in the eye.

I ran away and hid.

That afternoon we had our first gym lesson with **Mr McDool**. His name is **easy** to remember.

Mr McDool told us we were going to have our very own **class Olympics**. To make it seem more real, he even lit an old candle and called it the **Olympic torch**. He held it up high and some wax tipped out,

burning his armpits.

OUCH!

Mr McDool made ribbons to give out for first, second and third in the running races. I wish they had ribbons for **second last**.

I'm **really good** at coming **second last**.

I've learnt to hang back in the running heats. Don't line up along a bunch of guys who look fast. Line up near the end with the guys who look **slow**.

You can tell slow guys by a few sure-fire signs.

Socks pulled up too high.

Pants pulled up too high.

Finger always in nose.

Finger always in someone else's nose.

But usually the best way to tell who's the slowest is by finding the guy who's got the top bit of his **bum crack** showing. He's almost **always** going to be slow.

In my new class that kid's name was **Toby Hogan**. The others were calling him **Money Box** because it looked like his **bum crack** was a **coin slot**. He was the **perfect** choice to race with.

Well someone must have put a

hundred dollars

in the coin slot before Toby's heat, because it turned out

Toby Hogan was

super fast! 〉〉〉〉

← Me! Second last again!

We were standing around waiting for a row of girls to race when a kid called Josh Keenan started showing off his arm muscles. Before I knew what was happening, it turned into a **muscle contest**.

Great, another contest for me to come  in.

Or worse, **last!**

I tried to walk away but it was too late, it would've looked like I was **chickening out**. Everyone's muscles were going to be bigger than mine.

So when it was my turn, I did the

very best flex I could manage.

Toby Hogan

YOUR MUSCLES
ARE **HUGE**, WEIR!

WHOOO!

They didn't know I was doing
a trick that Dad showed me ...

It was going so well that I started **showing off** and turning so that all the **girls** could see.

That's when Toby Hogan saw what I was doing and **busted** me.

Then they all started **shouting**:

LIAR, LIAR, PANTS ON FIRE!

I thought they were just saying it cos it rhymes, but it turns out they weren't. I'd backed into **Mr McDool's Olympic torch** and my pants **really were**
on fire!

Mr McDool chucked a bucket of water on me to put it out.

There's that look again ... he's trying not to laugh!

I stood there **dripping wet** while my whole class, including *Bella Allen,* stared at me like I was a complete ...

weirdo.

The fire **burnt a hole** right in the middle of my school shorts. For the rest of the day I had to walk around sideways with my back to the wall so no-one could see my **frog** undies.

I couldn't wait till the bell at the end of the first day. When Mum came to pick me up, I ran to her as fast as I could.

When I ran past Bella she called out, **'Nice frogs!'**

UGH!

I went blank! Half my brain wanted to call back: **'Frogs are the best.'** The other half wanted to say: **'Frogs are the coolest.'** But it came out all wrong.

FROGS ARE THE BOOLEST!

ARGHHHHH!

Boolest! Who says **Boolest???!!!**

What a way to start the new year!

CHAPTER 4

The next day at school there was **awesome news.** Another new kid was starting. Since I had been there a **whole day already**, he was now the **new guy.**

And when he walked in, it got **even better.**

the new ~new~ guy!

I thought to myself, **YES!**

This guy makes me look **SUPER** normal!

He's going to take some of the attention off me ...

and I was right!

Henry quickly became the **strangest** guy in the class. He did everything a bit **differently**. Like when you said his name, it took three goes before he'd turn around.

HUH?

HENRY!
HENRY!!
HENRY!!!

And he has his own versions of nursery rhymes...

Mary had a little lamb,
Who one day just
dropped dead.
Now it goes to school
with her,
Between two chunks
of bread.

Well, the other kids think he's **strange**, but I think he's pretty **funny**.

That afternoon I found myself standing in line outside the PRINCIPAL's office. Henry was there too.

HI HENRY.

HENRY!

HENRY!

HI, WEIR!

PRINCIPAL

Turns out we were both there because of one guy ⟶ **Blake Green**. It hadn't taken us long to figure out that just about everything that Blake Green tells you to do, **you shouldn't do**.

When Blake first saw Henry he got the same look on his face that a dog gets when it looks at your ham sandwich.

dog

ham sandwich

Blake Green

Henry

Henry told me what Blake Green made him do. Henry was there because Blake tricked him into going into the **girls' toilets**.

HEY. WHERE DID MY
SCHOOL BAG GO?

IT'S OVER THERE.
GO HAVE A LOOK.

THANKS!

Here's what happened to **me**:

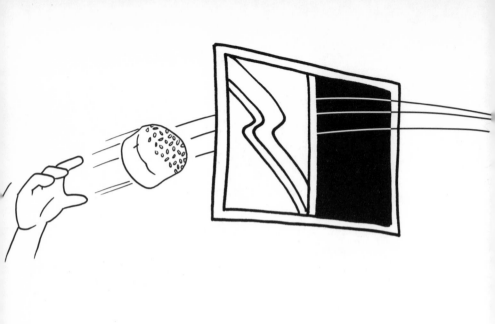

I managed to get **three** teachers angry
with **one** bread roll.

When it was my turn to go into the principal's office, Henry did something I **wasn't** expecting.

He helped me out!

So I thought I ought to help him out too.

HENRY WAS JUST LOOKING FOR HIS SCHOOL BAG. BLAKE TOLD HIM IT WAS IN THE TOILETS. HE DIDN'T REALISE IT WAS THE GIRLS' TOILETS. HE'S ONLY NEW.

We **grinned** at each other, both convinced that we were

<u>out</u>

of trouble.

We were <u>**wrong**</u>.

YOU'LL BOTH SPEND DETENTION WRITING A PAGE OF REASONS WHY YOU SHOULDN'T DO WHAT YOU DID AGAIN.

DANG!
I **hate** detention!

But when we walked in, I got the **best surprise** of my life!

Bella was in detention too! She was in trouble for accidentally elbowing the girl who gave her the **wet willy!**

Bella is easily the **prettiest** girl in the class. Well, whenever Jenny, Clare, Mary, Sue, Yana and Wendy are away.

Bella!

Jenny Clare Mary Sue Yana Wendy

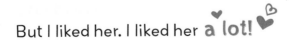

But I liked her. I liked her **a lot!**

And it turned out Henry liked her too!

As soon as we walked in, he tried out one of his **super smooth, talking-to-girls** tricks:

HI BELLA.
WANT TO HEAR
MY SPECIAL
NURSERY RHYME?

There was a little bunny,
Whose nose was very runny.
If you think it's very funny,
well, it's SNOT!

Bella moved away from Henry and closer to me.
That's when I realised that with Henry as my
sidekick, **I'd always be the cool one!**

cool one

So that's how me and Henry became

best friends.

CHAPTER 5

For the rest of the week me and Henry got up to **loads** of **funny business.**

I CAN MAKE YOU
FALL OVER WITH THE
POWER OF MY MIND.

Henry thinks my drawings are **cool**, so I've been making some **really funny** ones for him:

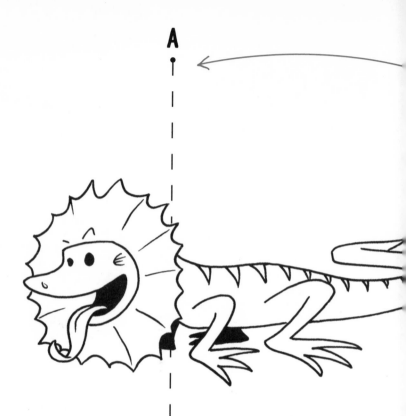

A

Frilled-neck | lizard

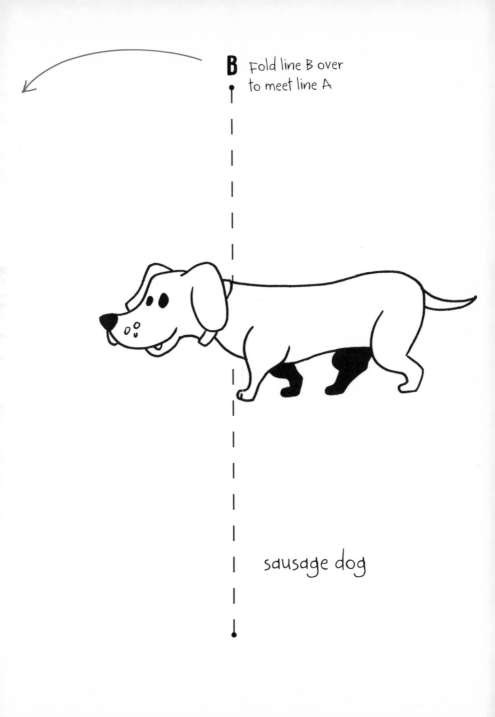

B Fold line B over
to meet line A

sausage dog

A

SKINK

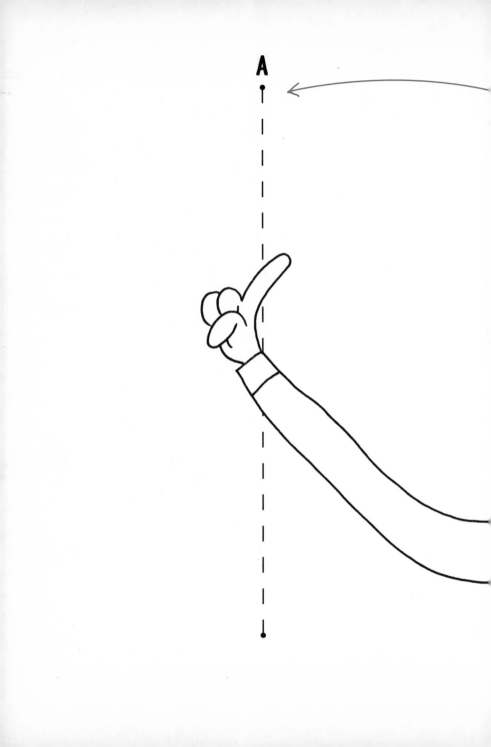

A

CHAPTER 6

The school principal, Mr Harris, came in to talk to our class about a **very important** matter.

'Kids, we've recently discovered that many of you have animals living in your hair, called **nits**.'

Animals living in my hair?! At first I thought:

HOW COOL!

But it turns out these things are not so good for you. They're tiny insects that **suck your blood** and make your head **itchy**.

Mr Harris then told us all to line up so some **nit inspectors** could check our heads.

I really hoped these guys didn't **check for worms** as well, because I wanted to keep my pants on.

They told us that if your head was **itchy**, it meant you probably had **nits**.

As soon as they said this, my head felt itchy, but I didn't want to scratch it. I think everyone felt the same. We all stood there with **itchy** heads that we were

too afraid to scratch!

At the end of it, Mr Harris told us that **we all had nits.**

The **whole** class!

We were each given a bottle of shampoo and told to stay home **(yay!)** until we'd really washed our hair.

Then he told us that these **creatures** were brought to school by someone carrying them in their hair, and it all started a few days ago.

Well, **of course** everyone right away turned to Henry. He'd just turned up a few days ago, and he had this **guilty** look on his face.

guilty

It **must've** been him!

I'd just made a new friend, and now he was the **nit guy!** I'd have to stay away from him . . .

It felt like this one time Mum let me choose a Transformer for Christmas, then she wrapped it up and I couldn't have it for a month!

Suddenly we heard some **chirping** noises in the classroom.

♪ meep meep ♫

At first I thought it was my **sister** hiding in the cupboard with the **hiccups**.

meep
meep

No-one knew what the noise was. So Miss Franklin told us all to go around the classroom and look for the **mysterious** noise.

We looked for ages, but **found nothing.**

Then Henry put up his hand.

MISS, IT SOUNDS LIKE BABY SPARROWS.

'How do you know that, Henry?' said Miss Franklin.

'We had **heaps** of birds on our farm, so I know what they sound like.'

'Do you know where they are?' the teacher asked.

'Sparrows like to nest up high,' said Henry. 'I think they're **in the ceiling**.'

Next, the school called some **bird inspectors** to come to our classroom and check the ceiling. And sure enough, **Henry was right**.

There was a nest up there, and not only that, it was the sparrows who were responsible for everyone's nits.

They found **heaps** of **bird lice** in the nest!

Henry became the

class hero for solving

The Mystery of the Chirping Noise

and everyone also realised that it wasn't him that gave us all nits.

All of a sudden I was **best friends** with the

coolest kid in the class.

The very next day Henry was back to being himself.

LOOK AT ME, I'M A WALRUS.

Oh well, at least I have him **all to myself again**.

CHAPTER 7

It was **show and tell** day, and I decided to take my **robotic ninja hamster** to school. He looked pretty dirty and needed a wash, so I turned on the tap and heard a **huge scream!**

Sally

EEEEEEEKK!

WHO TURNED ON THE TAP????

Sally was in the middle of a shower. Oops.
So when she came out, she got me back by
tying my school pants together.
When I went to put them on, I fell and
banged my head!

So I got her back by
putting glue in her shoes.

At school, Bella spent all of little lunch handing out invitations to her **birthday party**.

Everyone in my class got an invitation.

Everyone except me.

When she was handing them out and she got to me, she smiled and then walked right past.

She even gave one to Toby Hogan. She must have liked what he brought in for show and tell.

THIS IS WHAT YOU CALL A MONEY BOX.

Even **Henry** got an invitation!

Henry's toilet paper-dispensing helmet

WOOHOO!

What a bummer. She must have thought my **robotic ninja hamster** was weird. **Just like me.** Could this day get any **worse?**

After school I heard Mum on the phone talking to Bella's mum! Then Mum gave me the **worst news I could _ever_ hear.**

BELLA'S MUM HAS TO TAKE HER GRANDMA TO THE DOCTOR THIS AFTERNOON, SO BELLA IS COMING OVER TO OUR HOUSE. ISN'T THAT NICE?

NOOOOOOOO!!!

No-one's been over to my house yet. Not even Henry. **My family is _too_ weird!** But it was too late, and before I knew it,

Bella was at our front door.

'This is Weir's granddad, Bob,' said my mum.

HELLO THERE. HOW ABOUT A HUG FOR AN OLD MAN?

OH NO, I've seen him do this before!

ARHHH!
YOU'VE
BROKEN
MY MOUTH!

'Sorry about that, Bella!' said my mum.

'Just kidding!' said Granddad. 'They come out. Look. Isn't that cool?'

Then Granddad put his teeth in backwards and accidentally bit his tongue. He **screamed**.

AHHHHH!

Suddenly, there was another **loud scream**, coming from the bathroom.

OWWW!

UH OH. IT SOUNDS LIKE ROGER'S SLAMMED THE TOILET SEAT ON HIS **THING** AGAIN.

I don't like making stuff up, but in this case, **I had to.**

HE LIKES TO CALL HIS HAND A THING. LIKE RAHHHH, HAND THINGY.

My family is like one **disaster** waiting to happen after another!

Then my **worst fear** happened. Dad came home early from work. He walked right up to me and said the **baddest** thing he could say.

PULL MY FINGER!

DAD, NOOOOOO!!!

But it turns out he wasn't going to **embarrass** me after all.

PLEASE, I'VE GOT A CRAMP IN MY HAND!

So Mum gave Dad a quick hand massage.

Too many **close shaves** so far, but overall things were still alright.

Me and Bella were talking about the toys we'd brought in for show and tell. My **ninja hamster** was giving her **scientist doll** a ride on his back.

That's when Sally came out of her room.

Oh no, I forgot about the glue I put in her shoes!

She marched right up to where me and Bella were sitting.

SEE THOSE SHOES WEIR IS WEARING.
THEY'RE ACTUALLY **MY OLD SCHOOL SHOES.**

NOOOOOOO!

My life is
destroyed!

But then Bella said something that I didn't expect at all!

HEY. THATS KINDA COOL. MY SCHOOL BAG USED TO BELONG TO MY BROTHER.

HUH?

WOW. This is actually going great!

I was just starting to feel really good about things when the doorbell rang ... What now?!

I looked down the hallway and saw **Henry** at the door!

WHAT ARE YOU DOING, HENRY?

I'M WAITING FOR YOU TO LET ME IN!

'But why are you wearing **THAT?!**' I asked him.

'Because I have a co—'

AH-CHOO

OOO!

Henry's **big green booger** hit me in the eye!

I turned and accidentally **knocked Bella over.** That's when the **booger** flew from my face onto Bella's!

YUCK!

I tried to wipe it off her with Henry's toilet paper.

And that's when I spotted **Roger running down the hall** with Bella's doll!

I **panicked** and couldn't think properly. I turned to Bella and probably said the **un-coolest** thing you could say to a girl.

UH, ME
NEED GO
PEE-PEE
NOW!

I raced after Roger but by the time I got to his room, it was **too late**.

DOLL EAT CUSTARD.

The doll's head was covered in **yellow goop!**

What do I do now?!?!

Sally and Henry raced in after me.

QUICK, GET SOME WATER TO WASH HER!

I ran back out to the kitchen where Bella was sitting and filled up two cups of water. She looked at me **confused**.

UH. I LIKE TO
DRINK TWO
CUPS OF WATER
BEFORE I GO TO
THE TOILET . . .

IT HELPS ME
GO PEE-PEE.

OKAAAAAY.

When I got back to Roger's room, there was custard **everywhere**!

QUICK,
TO THE BATHROOM!

I grabbed the doll and ran to the bathroom. Sally and Henry followed.

Granddad was in there and we **squeezed** past him to get to the sink.

We were all hovering over the doll when Mum, Bella's mum and Bella walked in to see what all the **fuss** was about.

Granddad tried to explain...

WE FOUND A COUPLE OF **NITS** ON BELLA'S DOLL. SO WE'VE JUST GIVEN HER A LITTLE HAIR WASH WITH THIS **NIT SHAMPOO**.

We cleaned up the doll just in time to hand her back to Bella.

OH, THANK YOU FOR DOING THAT.

It was time to say bye to Bella, and I was sure she thought I was **even weirder** than before, thanks to my **crazy** family.

BYE WEIR. YOUR FAMILY IS **REALLY** FUNNY!

Then she pulled an envelope out of
her school bag.

It was an **invitation** to her birthday party,
that she'd drawn herself.

I LOVE **FROGS** TOO. I THINK THEY'RE THE **BOOLEST!**

Invitation

WOW!

A **special birthday invitation** from the **seventh-best-looking girl** at school.

This could be ...

MORE
TO COME!

For my three **favourite**

FROM ANH

WEirDos!

Xavier, Luc and Leon

ACKNOWLEDGEMENTS

FROM JULES

For all the kids with **nits**